"Go!" s

The Mario Bros. dash across the catwalks. With each step, the fragile bridges disintegrate behind them. They reach the far side simultaneously and skitter to a halt.

"That was close," pants Mario.

"Yeah, those collapsing bridges can be a real downer," replies Luigi.

"Very clever," says Mario, "but it may be your last joke."

A giant, hairy shadow moves over the scaffold as Donkey Kong lumbers toward them, carrying the largest barrel Mario has ever seen. The two plumbers inch backward to the edge of the girder. They feel the wind against their backs and the emptiness of the long drop behind them. Princess Toadstool looks on from behind the bars of her cage.

"Any ideas?" asks Mario desperately.

What will happen to the heroic plumbers now? It's up to you to make the decisions that will get them through the hairy times ahead!

Nintendo® Adventure Books:

DOUBLE TROUBLE
LEAPING LIZARDS
MONSTER MIX-UP
KOOPA CAPERS
PIPE DOWN!
DOORS TO DOOM

Available from ARCHWAY Paperbacks

Nintendo® ADVENTURE BOOKS
FEATURING THE SUPER MARIO BROS.®

DOORS TO DOOM
By Bill McCay

AN ARCHWAY PAPERBACK
Published by POCKET BOOKS
New York   London   Toronto   Sydney   Tokyo   Singapore

For Lary's Sarahs

AN ARCHWAY PAPERBACK *ORIGINAL*

An Archway Paperback published by
POCKET BOOKS, a division of Simon & Schuster
1230 Avenue of the Americas, New York NY 10020

ISBN: 0-671-74204-3

First Archway Paperback Printing October 1991

10   9   8   7   6   5   4   3   2   1

Creative Media Applications, Inc.
Series developed by Dan Oehlsen, Lary Rosenblatt & Barbara Stewart
Art direction by Fabia Wargin Design and Fred Gates
Cover painting by Greg Wray
Puzzle art by Josie Koehne
Edited by Eloise Flood

Special thanks to Ruth Ashby, Lisa Clancy, Paolo Pepe
& George Sinfield

Dear Game Player:

You are about to guide us through a great adventure. As you read this book, you will help us decide where to go and what to do. Whether we succeed or fail is up to you.

At the end of every chapter, you will make choices that determine what happens next. Special puzzles will help you decide what we should do—if you can solve them. The chapters in this book are in a special order. Sometimes you must go backward in order to go forward, if you know what we mean.

Along the way, you'll find many different items to help us with our quest. When you read that we have found something, such as a key, you'll see a box like the one below:

> ### ***Mario now has the key.***
> ### Turn to page 13.

Use page 121 to keep track of the things you collect and to keep score.

Good luck!
Driplessly yours,

The Super Mario Bros.

Clunk! Luigi awakens with a start. He sits up in bed and rubs his eyes as his bedroom materializes through a sleepy haze. In the corner is his newest invention, a subsonic pipe de-slimer. The smell of salami, the remains of last night's snack, wafts up from the bedside table.

The room is in the back of the Mario Bros. Plumbing Shop in Brooklyn, New York. Along with his older brother Mario, Luigi is a master plumber. But Mario and Luigi have a secret life. They are the chief heroes of the magical Mushroom Kingdom.

This world, below the surface of the earth, is populated by happy mushrooms and ruled by the Mushroom King and his daughter, Princess Toadstool. But a band of evil turtles and other monsters, led by King Bowser Koopa, is constantly trying to take over the kingdom. The Super Mario Bros. have been called to the rescue many times. They usually take the quickest way there, through the main pipe in their shop.

Thud! A dull noise comes from the hallway. Luigi climbs out of bed and heads for the door. He knows what to expect when he reaches it. Mario is sleepwalking again. "He's going to hurt himself," Luigi mumbles drowsily. "Or worse," he adds, snapping awake. "He'll break the new titanium-pipe wind surfer I left in the hall!" He rushes to the door.

"Whew! The wind surfer's okay," he says. But his brother is about to step into a pipe at the end of the hall—a pipe that wasn't there when they went to bed.

"Mario, stop!" Luigi shouts. He leaps down the hall and grabs Mario by his overalls straps just as the short round plumber takes a final step into the pipe.

"Gotcha!" exclaims Luigi.

Turn to page 51.

The door swings open. It's a jungle out there! A tropical wind blows Mario and Luigi through the door and slams it behind them. It disappears in a puff of smoke.

Twisted vines hang from platforms suspended in the air. Strange tropical plants grow thickly and there is a series of small islands in a blue lake. The plumbers are standing on a floating platform above one of the islands.

Mario kicks a pile of coconut shells at his feet. He stoops and picks up a large green key that was hidden under the pile.

"Hey, look! I wonder who left this here?" asks Mario as he reads the inscription on the key. "One side says, 'Positively Magic,' and the other says, 'Use once, then discard.'" He drops the key into his pocket.

Luigi leans against a tree and chews on a piece of grass. "Great. We have a key, now all we need is a door," he observes.

"Excuse me," says Mario politely, "but a Snapjaw is about to eat your head for lunch."

Luigi looks up to see the round green monster making its way down a vine near him.

"I think he brought a date," says Luigi, pointing to another Snapjaw descending a vine near Mario.

"Yikes! Let's vamoose!" shouts Mario. The Super Mario Bros. leap from the platform.

The Super Mario Bros. get 15 points.
Mario now has the key.
Turn to page 106.

"**H**old on. I'd love to get my hands on that Dr. Fungusnose," says Luigi.

"That's *Fungenstein*," mutters Mario.

Luigi goes on, "But we have to get to the top and complete our rescue mission. So let's skip this door. When I say three, jump for the scaffold."

"Gotcha." Mario nods.

"Three!" screams Luigi. Both plumbers fly through the air and land on a wide metal beam. Mario disappears along the girder in the fog. Luigi follows.

"Now, where's that ladder?" Mario says.

Luigi catches up just as Mario finds the ladder and begins to climb.

By the time they reach the top, the fog has almost lifted. Through the remains of the mist they can see the cage at the other end of the steel platform.

"That cage reminds me of Paulina," says

5

Mario. "Kong was forever kidnapping her and locking her up there." But the figure in the cage is not Paulina, Mario's old girlfriend. The pink dress and tiny gold crown belong to Princess Toadstool, the ruler—with her forgetful father—of the Mushroom Kingdom.

"Where's Donkey Kong?" wonders Luigi. The great ape is nowhere to be seen.

"Don't ask," advises Mario. "Let's free the princess and get out of here."

"But where could you hide a thousand-pound ape up here?" Luigi persists.

Suddenly, a door appears just beyond the cage. It swings open and a giant hairy figure lumbers onto the scaffolding.

"I told you not to ask questions," says Mario sarcastically. "Now I'll take care of Donkey Breath once and for all."

"That's *Donkey Kong,*" corrects Luigi.

Mario rushes toward his old nemesis.

The Super Mario Bros. get 10 points.
Turn to page 8.

"Me Tarzan, you Cheetah," replies Luigi as he reaches out and grabs the vine.

He swings through the air and almost reaches the platform. But the vine is too short. The daring young plumber on the flying trapeze swings back toward Mario.

"Nooo!" Mario screams as Luigi collides with him, knocking them both from the vines.

They tumble down through the jungle, battered by vines and leaves as they fall. They land in a pile of rotten banana peels.

As they try to stand in the slippery mess, a giant Snapjaw descends on both of them.

"Lunch!" is the last thing they hear.

Game Over!

"**H**ey, wait a second!" Mario says. He abruptly halts his assault on Donkey Kong.

The top level of the ape's scaffolding has changed since Mario was here last. The only way to reach the cage and Donkey Kong is to cross one of two catwalks.

The two paths twist and turn toward the trapped princess and her hairy captor. Both look quite rickety.

Luigi comes up behind Mario. "Which one do we take?" he asks.

Mario examines the catwalks closely, then turns to Luigi. "It's obvious," he says. "We take the shortest route."

The two brothers talk it over. Then they take a few steps back and start running at full speed toward the catwalks.

Solve the puzzle below to see what happens next:

• Study the drawing of the two catwalks carefully, and find the shortest route.

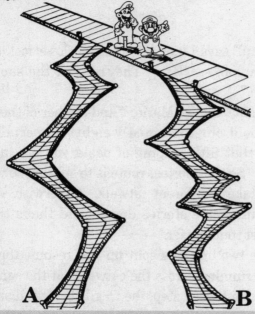

A   B

✕ **If you think catwalk A is shorter, turn to page 118.**

✳ **If you think catwalk B is shorter, turn to page 106.**

✳ **If you think both catwalks are the same length, turn to page 10.**

9

6

"**S**top!" says Luigi. He takes a closer look at the catwalks. "Hey! They're both the same length."

"Right," replies Mario. "And neither of them will hold our combined weight. Especially after that fifth helping of pasta you ate last night. So the shortest route is to split up so we each take a different catwalk. Otherwise, we end up twelve stories down—and that's the longest route by far."

The two brothers split up and resume their dash, running across the catwalks at the same time. With each step, the fragile bridges disintegrate behind them. They reach the other side simultaneously and skitter to a halt.

"That was close," pants Mario.

"Yeah, I hate those collapsing bridges. They can be a real downer," replies Luigi.

"Very clever," says Mario, "but it may be your last joke."

A giant shadow moves over them as they stand on the edge of the scaffolding.

"Is it getting dark in here?" asks Luigi.

"I knew it wouldn't be the last joke," sighs Mario.

The giant ape lumbers toward them carrying the largest barrel Mario has ever seen. The two plumbers inch backward to the edge of the girder. They feel the wind against their backs and the emptiness of the long drop behind them.

"Any ideas?" asks Mario desperately.

"When I say *now*, we both jump him," responds Luigi.

"That's your idea? We jump a thousand-pound gorilla? No wonder you never finished World 7 on Subcon."

Luigi shrugs. "We might as well go down fighting," says the younger plumber. "Maybe one of us will make it and save her Highness."

The princess looks on from behind the bars of her cage.

The ferocious simian takes a final step forward and lets out a tremendous roar.

"Let's go for it," says Mario. The two brothers squat down and prepare to tackle their enemy. But before they can act, a door appears in midair behind them. Mario and Luigi look at the door, then at Donkey Kong, and back at the door again.

The sudden appearance of the door causes Donkey Kong to hesitate for an instant.

"Do we take the door and leave the princess, or do we fight and hope one of us is left to save her?" asks Luigi.

The giant ape flexes his muscles and prepares to slam the barrel down on them.

"We don't have a choice," says Mario.

If you think the Mario Bros. should jump through the door, turn to page 21.

If you think they should fight Donkey Kong, turn to page 78.

7

"**S**tick with me," shouts Mario over his shoulder. "And do exactly as I tell you. This rig can be tricky and this is your first time. We don't want a Game Over before we reach that overgrown hairball."

"I always do what you say, big brother," replies Luigi, crossing his fingers and toes.

Mario and Luigi reach the next level and jump over a barrel in unison. They climb ladders and leapfrog over barrels as they make their way up the scaffolding.

As they pause to catch their breath, Luigi looks down. "We're about to become crispy critters!" he yells. Mario glances down to see great balls of fire rising toward them from a flaming oil can.

"That ape burns me up," he says. He takes a deep breath and rushes up the next ladder. Luigi races after him.

The assault of barrels and fireballs becomes

more and more furious as the two plumbers approach the top. With Mario leading the way, they jump, dodge, and climb up the steel girders and ladders. Finally, they come to a junction in the scaffolding where the structure twists and turns in a complex maze of steel.

Without hesitation, Mario starts up the maze, taking the path to the right. Luigi pauses and stares at the girders.

"What are you waiting for?" shouts the older plumber over the din of rolling barrels and the constant *whoosh* of fireballs.

"The left path is the right path!" shouts Luigi. "I know you're older, and you've been here before, but take a minute and look ahead."

Mario starts to argue with his younger brother, then takes a closer look at the scaffolding.

Solve the puzzle on the opposite page and help the Mario Bros. decide which is the correct path:

• Find the route to the top that uses the smallest number of ladders and crosses the fewest barrels. The Mario Bros. cannot cross over the fireballs.

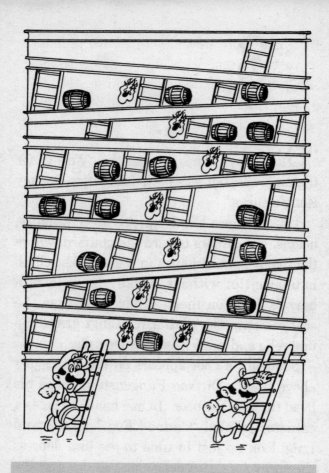

The Super Mario Bros. get 10 points.

If Luigi is on the correct path, turn to page 24.

If Mario is on the correct path,
turn to page 118.

8

"**O**kay," says Mario reluctantly. "We'll go for the umbrella, but let's move fast before Donkey Kong returns."

The brothers climb quickly over ladders, beams, and girders toward the platform where the magic parasol hangs in midair. The climb is uneventful without Donkey Kong to rain barrels down on them. They jump from the scaffold onto the platform. Luigi grabs the umbrella and tucks it into his overalls.

Suddenly, a door appears on the girder just above them. Dr. Von Fungenstein pokes his head through the door. In one hand, he holds a canister labeled "Canned Fog." Mario and Luigi look up just in time to see him depress the spray nozzle. A dense mist settles over the platform.

The fog is so thick that Mario and Luigi can barely see the ends of their mustaches. The evil doctor's laughter echoes in the murk.

Mario leaps toward the sound. He lands on the girder just outside the door and jams his boot into the door as it closes.

"Yeow!" he yells as the door slams on his toes. His scream guides Luigi through the fog to the doorway.

"That's using your brains," says Luigi.

"Be quiet and help me get this door open," says Mario indignantly. The two plumbers open the door with a mighty shove.

If you think Mario and Luigi should keep going toward the top, turn to page 5.

If you think they should jump through the door after Dr. Von F., turn to page 85.

The Super Mario Bros. get 10 points.

Luigi now has the parasol.

9

"This may be our only chance to get Dr. Fungushead," says Luigi.

"That's *Fungenstein*," groans Mario. "So get going already."

Luigi climbs up onto Mario's shoulders, plants his left boot on his brother's ear, and pushes himself through the door.

"Ouch!" yells Mario. He clenches his teeth and scrambles through the doorway, dropping with a thud on top of his brother.

"Oof!" says Luigi.

They stand up together and look around. Dr. Von Fungenstein is nowhere in sight.

"This is Subcon!" gasps Mario.

"Yeah," says Luigi. "Land of Dreams."

The Super Mario Bros. get 10 points.
Turn to page 85.

10

Luigi catches up to Mario just as he opens the door. The two plumbers step through the door together.

They are greeted by thunderous applause. The ceremonial hall of the Mushroom Palace, into which they have stepped, is filled to the rafters with mushroom nobles.

Luigi looks at Mario and his jaw drops. His brother's usual red overalls have been transformed into red satin formal plumber's attire, complete with pipe-wrench cummerbund and diamond plumber's-helper cuff links.

"Dahling, you look mahvelous," says Luigi.

"You look pretty good yourself," responds Mario. Luigi is similarly dressed, in a green outfit.

The applause dies down and is replaced by the royal mushroom march. Two mushroom guards appear from the wings of the stage. They escort the nattily-clad plumbers down to the center of the stage.

On the stage the Mushroom King and his court await. Dr. Von Fungenstein stands to one side, smiling.

Princess Toadstool steps to the podium and reads a royal proclamation declaring Mario and Luigi recipients of the Order of the Golden Mushroom for unrivaled heroism, bravery, ingenuity, moral character, and overall good looks.

The ceremony takes hours, and the party afterwards lasts for days.

Game Over. You Win!

11

The door swings open and the landscape of Subcon stretches before them. As Mario and Luigi jump through the door, it disappears behind them in a flash, singeing the back of Mario's red overalls.

"I hate it when that happens," grumbles Mario.

The Mario Bros. stand beside a waterfall and a large pond. Barrels bob on the water's surface. As they have done many times before, they start to cross over the pond leaping from barrel to barrel.

Halfway across, a door opens in the middle of the waterfall. Dr. Von Fungenstein pokes his bald head through the door in the flowing water.

"You're not so smart after all," he shouts at the plumbers as they balance themselves on the barrels.

A horde of pink Beezos rises over a nearby

hill and begins a slow swoop toward the Mario Bros.

At the same time, all the barrels except the one they are standing on begin to sink into the water. The barrels bob up and down in a rhythmic pattern.

"Should we stay here, or try to make it to shore?" asks Mario.

"That depends on the way the barrels bob up and down," replies Luigi. "If we can make it by jumping on them, we should run. Otherwise we should stay put and duck."

Solve the puzzle on the next page to see what happens next:

• The barrels move up and down one space every second except that they stay on the surface for two seconds. Decide if Mario and Luigi can make it to the other side of the pond.

The Super Mario Bros. get 15 points.

If you think Mario and Luigi should run,
turn to page 39.

If you think Mario and Luigi should duck,
turn to page 88.

12

Mario decides to trust Luigi's judgment. "Maybe you're right," he says.

"Trust me, big brother, this is the best way up," says Luigi.

They begin climbing with Luigi in the lead. Following his route, they traverse the maze with ease. But as Mario climbs onto the next level of the scaffold, the ladder below him breaks away.

"You were right about the route," says Mario. "But now we're stuck on this level."

Luckily, the overhanging girders deflect the barrels and fireballs the giant ape is still hurling, giving the brothers a chance to rest and plan their next move.

"Maybe we aren't so stuck after all," says Luigi, pointing down at his feet. Between his boots is a small latch neatly tucked into the floor of the girder.

"Take a look at this," he says, pulling up on the latch. "It must be one of Dr. Von Fungusbrain's doors."

"That's *Fungenstein,*" Mario corrects.

The door leads to another level of the scaffolding, far below. A faint voice drifts up through the opening. The voice sounds very far away, but the message is clear. It's a cry for help!

As the two plumbers strain to hear the voice, they notice an elevator coming up the scaffolding, within jumping distance.

"This door could be a trap," says Luigi. "That's a long drop and we don't know what's down there."

"But we can't ignore a cry for help," Mario objects.

If you think the Mario Bros. should take the elevator, turn to page 36.

If you think they should take the trapdoor, turn to page 119.

13

"**Y**ou're right," says Luigi apologetically. "Everyone deserves a second chance. Even large green toads who've turned into skateboard freaks."

Mario tries to reason with the irate skateboarding toad. "Luigi was only kidding," he says pleasantly. "Let's talk this over."

Wart's smile fades and he reverts to his old, disgustingly mean self. He reaches down and picks up his skateboard and launches it at the two plumbers.

As the skateboard whizzes by, Mario and Luigi jump onto its broad deck. They both duck low and whiz out the Dutch door. Mario grabs the nose of the board and leans left. The board makes a sharp turn and zooms down the hall with the two plumbers aboard.

Luigi looks at his brother and smiles. "Most excellent maneuver, Dude!"

Mario looks back proudly. When he turns

around again, he's facing a rapidly-approaching door at the end of the hall. *Kuh-rash!*

As the two brothers get to their feet, they hear Wart's angry screams close behind. They push the door open and tumble onto an open-air path. They slam the door behind them and frantically pull up turnips to block it from opening.

The barricade holds at least temporarily. They hear Wart pounding on the door from the other side. But it stays shut.

"Let's bug out of here," says Luigi.

"Yeah, before we get swallowed by that bug-eating reptile," adds Mario.

The Mario Bros. scamper down the path. They finally halt in front of an enormous garage door.

The Super Mario Bros. get 15 points.
Turn to page 114.

14

Luigi reaches for the lower knob and swings the bottom half of the door open. Music blares at them. Mario ducks and follows his brother through the opening.

They stand up inside a familiar, but changed cave. Wart, the toad prince, sits on a pedestal in the middle of the room. The giant toad is wearing a multi-colored Hawaiian shirt, Walktoad headphones, jams, and sunglasses. He is munching on a corn dog and playing with a Game Boy. A very large yellow skateboard with irridescent green wheels is propped against the pedestal. The cave is decorated with posters of skateboard champions in acrobatic poses.

Mario and Luigi tense as the giant toad turns toward them. He opens his mouth and Luigi gets ready to leap.

"Yo, Plumboids!" says Wart. "You dudes should check out this new vid-game—it's truly radical."

Mario and Luigi look at each other, stunned. Could this be the same Wart that took over Subcon with his dream machine and caused so much trouble the last time they were here?

Luigi is speechless, so Mario takes over. "Most bodacious!" says the older plumber, as Luigi stares at him in amazement. "Where did you learn to skateboard, Dude?"

"Right here in the Land of Outrageous Dreams. It's a most excellent dream, Dude. Far superior to that conquer-the-world stuff," pipes the green skateboard demon. "Now I dream of skating the most radical incline possible. That short fungus doctor dude helped me turn Subcon into this raucous skate park. Gnarly, don't you agree?"

"Excellent," says Mario. "I'll translate later," he adds under his breath to Luigi.

The giant toad continues, "Hey, Plumber Dudes, those hats are most outrageous. Let's make a minor trade. You give me a hat and I give you this very electronic garage door opening device."

"Did I understand that correctly?" asks Luigi. "He wants to trade a garage door opener for one of our hats?"

"Most correct," replies Mario. "Give him your hat. We could use that garage door opener later."

"My hat?" replies Luigi. "Your head is much bigger. Give him your hat."

"I'm sure you have the most outrageously bulbous braincase," retorts Mario. "Turn over your head gear."

"Not so fast, big brother, let me remind you of a few facts that prove whose head is bigger. If my head is bigger, then I'll give him my hat, but if I can prove you're the one with the swollen pate, you give him your hat. Agreed?"

"Whatever you say," replies Mario. "But what's a 'pate'?"

Solve this puzzle to see what happens next:

• Help Mario and Luigi decide whose head is bigger by following Luigi's logic.

• The facts below relate to Luigi, Mario, the king, and Princess Toadstool. Read them carefully and deduce who has the biggest head.

1. Everyone who is related has opposite traits.

2. We already know that Luigi is the tallest and Mario is the shortest.

3. Either Mario or Luigi has the largest hat size.

4. No one in the family of the one with the biggest head is the smartest, but the one with the biggest head is related to the loudest one.

5. The one who eats the most is related to the smartest one and is the same sex as the one who is quietest.

6. The smartest one is shorter than the loudest.

The Super Mario Bros. get 15 points.

✳ If you think Mario has the bigger head, turn to page 69.

✳ If you think Luigi has the bigger head, turn to page 94.

15

The two plumbers climb onto the final platform and look around.

"Everything looks the same as I remember it," says Mario. "There are the vines, the piles of coconuts, and the large cage with a hulking monster inside."

"Hey!" exclaims Luigi. "That hulking monster is Bowser Koopa, king of the turtles, and the most despicable creature in all the mushroom worlds."

"How did he get here?" asks Mario as they walk over to the cage.

The large green turtle rushes to the side of the cage nearest them and starts talking rapidly. "Am I glad to see you guys!" he exclaims. "One minute I'm in my castle thinking about how I'm going to . . . Never mind what I was thinking. Anyway, the next thing I know, I'm locked in this cage in the middle of who knows where, and then you guys show up and boy, am

I glad to see you! Get me out of here."

"Slow down, Bowser, old turtle," says Mario. "We don't want to make any hasty decisions that we might all regret."

"You've got to let me out," pleads the rotten reptile. "Do it for old times' sake. On second thought, do it in spite of old times' sake."

Luigi walks over to the cage door. "Look at this." He points to the padlock.

The lock is labeled, "'Insert green key and turn.'"

Before Mario can respond, Dr. Von Fungenstein appears in a doorway at the end of the platform, just beyond the cage. The doctor slams the door behind him.

Luigi starts to say something, but he's distracted by a movement at the other end of the platform. He and Mario turn to see Donkey Kong Jr. lumbering toward them.

If Mario has the key, turn to page 59.
If Mario doesn't have the key, turn to page 42.

16

"As much as I would like to, we can't leave even you in the clutches of that hairy ape," says Mario to Bowser. "But you'd better do all those things you said you would."

"Oh, I will," replies the evil king of the turtles, crossing his heart.

Mario inserts the key in the padlock and quickly unlocks Bowser's cage. The huge green turtle smiles slyly as he shoves the cage door open. "Thanks, suckers," he says, laughing. "While that big ape takes care of you, I'm out of here."

He bolts from the cage and takes two steps before he slips on a banana peel and slides directly into Donkey Kong Jr.

The two titans struggle. Bowser glares over his shoulder at Mario as Junior twists his shell. "You did that on purpose," he screams in a voice that can be heard all the way to Brooklyn.

Before Mario can reply, the turtle king and Donkey Kong Jr. roll off the platform and plummet into the jungle below.

"So much for good deeds to turtles," comments Mario. "Now what do we do?"

Luigi pulls the key out of the lock and reads the inscription again. "Use once, then discard." He throws the key at the door.

To his surprise, the door swings open onto a long dark passageway with an eerie green glow at the end of it. The two brothers look at each other. "This looks like the only way out," says Mario.

"But it doesn't look like it goes to Brooklyn," protests Luigi.

The Super Mario Bros. get 10 points.
Turn to page 45.

17

The plumbers make their decision, and jump for the lift. Fireballs whiz by them and bounce off the steel beams.

A flaming sphere careens toward the brothers. They immediately jump from the elevator to a beam, then race along the scaffold and jump to another elevator.

Mario looks around. "Now we've done it," he moans. "There's no way off this lift!"

Luigi lies down on his back and closes his eyes. "In that case, wake me when we get to the top," he says.

"I always knew you were laid back," says Mario, "but this is ridiculous. You'd better wake up and smell the Draino. This elevator is headed straight for the top and we're going to be flattened into a couple of plumber pepperoni slices."

Luigi hops to his feet, horrified.

As they move up, Mario's old nemesis,

Donkey Kong, comes into view. But Luigi takes little notice of the monster. His eyes focus on the cage next to the ape. There behind the bars is a lone figure in a pink dress and a small gold crown.

Luigi taps Mario on the shoulder and points upward. "There's Princess Toadstool. It looks like Dr. Von Fungusfoot wasn't lying about transporting people from one place to another."

"That's *Fungenstein*," Mario says irritably. "And . . . hey! It is the Princess!"

The giant ape paces back and forth beside the princess's cage, occasionally throwing barrels at the plumbers.

The lift carries Mario and Luigi closer and closer to the top of the scaffold. "We'd better think of something soon," says Luigi. "I'd hate for the princess to see the Super Mario Bros. turned into mush. It might change her otherwise high opinion of us."

The Super Mario Bros. get 15 points.
Turn to page 82.

Turn to page 82.

18

"We have to give him the correct answer," says Luigi. "If we don't get off this elevator, we have no chance of coming back to save the princess."

Mario agrees reluctantly. "There are more than twenty," he shouts. "Now let us jump through the door."

"With pleasure," replies Dr. Von F.

The elevator shakes as the whole scaffold starts to come apart at the seams.

Mario and Luigi jump through the door onto solid ground. They turn and see the scaffolding flying to pieces. As Princess Toadstool shoots past, they reach out to catch her. But before they get back inside the door, a thousand pounds of angry ape crashes onto their heads.

Game Over!

19

"Let's make like Beezos and buzz off," says Mario. As the first barrel surfaces, he leaps onto it. Before it can sink, he is airborne again and headed for the shore. Luigi waits for the barrels to realign themselves, then takes them in the same pattern.

The Beezos whir past. Before the brightly clad buzzers can regroup, Mario and Luigi disappear over a hill.

The speedy plumbers leap a large crevasse, then come to a halt at the base of a large jar. They look up at the intricate pattern painted on the side of the pottery. "I think we should jump inside and check it out."

"We'll probably find a Phanto in there," Luigi reminds Mario. "Those red and white devils will chase you forever."

The sound of Beezos rises above the hillside.

"The jar is the best place to hide until those bee brains buzz off," says Mario.

"I say we hide behind it until the coast is clear," suggests Luigi. "Phantos give me the creeps!"

Luigi stares intently at the painting on the jar. It depicts a group of Subconian creatures. The drawing is divided in half. Each side appears to be the mirror image of the other.

"It's a Subcon Game Jar!" exclaims Luigi. "I've always wanted to find one. We have find the difference between the two sides."

"Great!" says Mario. "Then we find a warp zone or something, right?"

"No," replies Luigi. "It's just for fun."

"You want to play a game now?" says his brother in disbelief.

"Sure," says Luigi. "I never pass up a good game. Just give me a couple of minutes."

Solve the Game Jar puzzle on the next page for fun, then decide what Mario and Luigi should do next:

• The two drawings are mirror images of each other, except that one creature is out of place. Can you figure out which one?

After a few minutes Luigi turns to Mario and smiles. "I got it," he says proudly. "Now, where were we?"

"We were trying to decide whether to hide in the jar or behind it," says Mario, urgently pointing to a swarm of Beezos rising above the hill.

The Super Mario Bros. get 15 points.

If Mario and Luigi hide behind the jar, turn to page 63.

If they jump into the jar, turn to page 71.

20

Mario and Luigi race toward the new door. Luigi tests the latch. It's unlocked.

"I think these two want to be alone," he says to Mario.

"You're right. How thoughtless of us," replies Mario. He grins at Bowser.

"Have fun," says Mario. Luigi opens the door and the Mario Bros. leap through.

They hear a medley of growls, yells, and laughter as they slam the door shut.

"I love doing a good deed," says Mario.

"Me too," says Luigi. "And no one deserved that deed more than Bowser."

"Yeah," says Mario. "But that door didn't take us back to Brooklyn."

The Super Mario Bros. get 10 points.
Turn to page 85.

21

Mario inserts the key in the door and gives it a turn. The two plumbers plunge through and slam the door shut.

They are standing in an open landscape of swaying palm trees and beautiful green hills. Above them the sun burns brightly.

"It looks like Dr. Von Fungustoes did it to us again," says Luigi.

"That's *Fungenstein!*" screams Mario.

"Whatever." Luigi waves a hand. "But this definitely *isn't* Brooklyn."

The Super Mario Bros. get 15 points.
Turn to page 85.

22

"There are more than twenty," says Luigi very quietly to his brother. "But that was too easy. I don't trust this guy."

"Did I mention the special bonus?" calls the evil scientist. "If you answer correctly, I'll destroy the scaffold, Donkey Kong and all."

"What if we get it wrong?" asks Mario.

"You might say, I leave you flat," the spiteful doctor chuckles.

Mario whispers to his brother, "If the scaffold comes down, it will destroy the princess as well as Donkey Kong."

The Super Mario Bros. get 15 points.

If you think Mario and Luigi should give the correct answer, turn to page 38.

If you think they should give the incorrect answer, turn to page 109.

23

The brothers step into the passage. Their surroundings are transformed into a long tunnel that ascends a steep incline, like a giant ramp. The floor curves up into the walls, forming one continuous surface. Although the tunnel is dimly lit, Luigi notices that it's marked with pairs of black lines that weave up the walls, drop to the floor, then snake up the walls again.

"What do you suppose made those lines?" he asks Mario. "I don't know of anything in Subcon that makes marks like that. They look almost like wheel tracks."

"Let's find out," says Mario. "I have a hunch that we're in for some gnarly business before this adventure is over."

They trudge up the ramp into the green glow. When they reach the top, the tunnel dead-ends onto a small platform. Against the wall are two doors, each guarded by a Ninji.

The small black-clad creatures bounce up and down in place.

"Check out their T-shirts," says Mario. Emblazoned on the creatures' T-shirts is a giant green toad and bright red letters that say, "Right&Wrong Brothers."

Luigi taps Mario on the shoulder. "I've heard about these Ninjis. One always tells the truth and the other always lies. But I don't know which is which."

Between the bouncing Right&Wrong Brothers is a sign. Mario squints to read it in the dim light. "'Doorman on duty,'" he says. "'To open a door, just ask.'"

"Something tells me that if we go through the wrong door, it means big trouble," says Luigi.

Mario agrees. "So what do we do now?"

"It's simple. We ask them which door to go through," says Luigi calmly.

"How do we know which one is telling the truth?" asks Mario, a bit perplexed.

Luigi rubs his chin. "We have to ask the question just right. It's one of two choices, but I'm not sure which one."

Solve this puzzle to help Mario and Luigi continue their adventure:

• These are the two questions that Luigi remembers. Decide which is the correct one to ask the Right&Wrong Brothers, in order to find out which door to choose.

Question 1: "Which door would you choose if it were up to you?"

Question 2: "What would you say if I asked, 'is this the correct door?'"

✕ If you think question #1 is correct, turn to page 112.

✳ If you think question #2 is correct, turn to page 56.

24

" 'BOSS BUFONIDAE,' eh?" says Mario.

"What does bufonidae mean?" asks Luigi.

"It . . . well . . . oh, come on, Luigi, do I have to spell it out? Everyone knows what bufonidae means," Mario huffs.

"Just testing you," Luigi says quickly. "Now, then, I'll twist the bolts in the same direction and . . . presto!"

The large jar rattles on its base. Then it shakes violently and begins to roll around on its edge. Mario and Luigi jump backward.

Finally the urn settles. In a twinkle of magic light, the door opens. Beyond it is a dank, dark tunnel. The musty stench of old laundry and rotten grass clippings floats out. An eerie green light seems to emanate from the walls themselves.

Luigi peers into the green gloom, trying to see what lies ahead.

Mario steps up to the doorway and smiles.

"This is the secret shortcut I was looking for," he says. "I told you it was through the jar," he adds proudly.

"You said the shortcut was in the jar," Luigi reminds him.

"I'm sure this is the way we want to go," says Mario as he steps into the passageway. "Let's get started."

"Hold it," interjects Luigi. "I think we should take a look inside the jar first."

"What happened to your fear of Phantos?" asks Mario.

"My fear of deadend tunnels is greater!" says Luigi. "Let's see what the jar holds."

If you think Mario and Luigi should enter the passage, turn to page 45.

If you think they should jump into the jar, turn to page 71.

25

The top knob turns easily in Luigi's hand. He pulls the door open with one swift motion.

A giant woofer stares the Mario Bros. in the face. The sound from it is deafening. Luigi tries to slam the door shut, but the vibrations from the enormous speaker blast him and Mario against the opposite wall.

They are trapped by the sound of a squealing bass guitar. They struggle to recover, but are assaulted by a drum solo that shakes them to their bones.

The vibrations become unbearable as the keyboard kicks in and rocks them relentlessly. Luckily, they black out before the final guitar riff.

Game Over!

26

Gotcha! Gotcha! Gotcha! The word echoes against the pipe walls as Luigi and Mario tumble head over plunger through the darkness. The tall thin Luigi lands with a thud on top of his sibling.

Mario comes to with a groan as Luigi untangles himself and struggles to his feet. "That's the last time I save you from sleepwalking," Luigi scolds.

"Did you get the number of that truck?" mumbles Mario, staggering upright.

The two brothers look around. They are in a square, dimly lit room made of gray stone blocks. The walls extend upward into darkness. There are no doors, pipes, stairways, or other escape routes visible.

The sound of a squeaking hinge makes both plumbers look up. High above them, well beyond jumping range, a door opens. Light pours into the chamber. In the doorway stands a short, round figure in a white lab coat. His oversized feet protrude from beneath the coat and extend beyond the edge of the doorway.

Although the figure has the squat shape of a Goomba, his head is larger and rounder than the typical Goomba's, making him look almost intelligent. Tufts of hair protrude from both sides of his otherwise bald scalp. But the beady eyes and large mouth leave no doubt that this is a member of the rogue mushroom clan.

As Mario and Luigi stare at the strange Goomba, he chuckles.

"Welcome," he says in a crackly little voice. "I'm so glad you dropped in."

"Very funny," shouts Mario.

"Let me introduce myself," says the strange little mushroom. "I am Dr. Sporis Von Fungenstein, the greatest scientist in the Mushroom Kingdom and its next ruler."

The Mario Bros. stare in disbelief.

The mad Goomba scientist continues. "I plan to conquer all the mushroom worlds—and make a few bucks on the side."

"Doesn't everyone?" asks Luigi sarcastically.

"But my plan is infallible," croaks Dr. Von

Fungenstein. "I have an irresistible recipe for mushroom and turtle soup which I plan to sell in a chain of fast food restaurants. There's real money in fast food."

Mario and Luigi can't believe their ears. Luigi squints up at the strange little creature. "You think you can defeat the Mushroom King and Bowser Koopa and turn their subjects into fast food?"

"I've already started," says the mad scientist. "With my secret weapon, I can make new passageways into all of the known mushroom worlds. My Doors to Doom Machine can send the inhabitants of one world into another and thereby get rid of them forever. I have already taken care of almost everyone who can stop my plan. You two are the last. And now, you've fallen into my little trap."

"Let me guess," says Mario. "You brought us here to make plumber sauce to spice up your soup?"

"Not exactly," cackles Von Fungenstein.

With that, the lunatic scientist turns on his heels and slams the door. Crazed laughter echoes above them.

The Mario Bros. look at each other in disbelief as two doors materialize on the other side of the tiny room. One door is white and the other is black. Then they take a closer look at the floor. It's made of alternating black and white square blocks. It looks like a checkerboard.

"This is where we blow this joint," Mario remarks, stepping onto the next block. He is immediately thrown back to his original position by a mysterious force.

After some experimentation, the Super Mario Bros. discover that they can move across the checkered floor, but they have to jump in an L-shaped pattern. They can jump two squares up and one across or one square up and two across. They can move left, right, backward, or forward, but they have to take turns moving.

The only way to open either door is for both Mario and Luigi to land on the square in front of it.

Solve the puzzle below to help Mario and Luigi decide which door to take:

The Super Mario Bros. get 10 points.

If Mario and Luigi take the white door, turn to page 92.

If they take the black door, turn to page 101.

27

"Now I remember," says Luigi. "It's a little complicated, but if we ask each Ninji what he would say, the one that always tells the truth is going to tell us the truth, but the one who always lies will lie about lying and wind up telling us the truth."

"Just ask the question," says Mario. "I hate it when you get logical."

Luigi poses the question to the Ninji in front of the left door. The left Right&Wrong Brother frowns and says in a squeaky voice, "I'd say this is the wrong door."

Next Luigi turns to the right Right&Wrong Brother and asks the same question. He replies in an equally squeaky voice, "I'd say this is the right door."

Luigi smiles. "I told you," he says triumphantly. "We take the right door."

The Ninji in front of the right door turns the latch and opens the door. The passage beyond is even more dark and dank than they one the are in. Mario recognizes the ominous tunnel immediately.

"This leads to Wart's cave," says Mario. "I hope you brought along some vegetables."

Mario and Luigi step through the door and start down the passage. As Luigi goes by, the Ninji holds out its stubby hand. The tall plumber rolls his eyes and digs into his pocket to find a gold coin. He tips the Ninji and steps through the door.

The Mario Bros. move through the dimly lit tunnel. It's covered with graffiti. Mario turns to study the tunnel art. But Luigi taps him on the shoulder. "Listen," he says.

"That sounds like music," says Mario.

The two plumbers move down the passage. The music grows louder and louder. Finally they come to a doorway in the wall of the tunnel. It's a Dutch door painted day-glow red on top and fluorescent green on the bottom. Above it is a sign that says 'SKATE OR CROAK'. A rock-and-roll song from the sixties blares from behind the door.

As Mario and Luigi try to decide what to do, a hatch opens in the ceiling of the tunnel. The brothers look up at the smiling face of Dr. Von Fungenstein as he pokes his head through the opening.

"I'll make this easy for you," says the doctor. "Just turn the knob and step inside." Then he slams the trapdoor shut.

Mario and Luigi face the Dutch door again. Naturally, there are two doorknobs on the door, one on the top half and one on the bottom half.

"Just turn the knob," repeats Mario in a frustrated voice. "I'd like to turn that fungus's knob."

Luigi studies the door. "Let's take a chance," he says as he reaches out.

If you think Luigi should turn the top doorknob, turn to page 50.

If you think he should turn the bottom door-knob, turn to turn to page 28.

28

Mario steps quickly to the door and reads a sign below the handle. The sign says, "Insert green key in lock to exit.'"

He looks at the inscription on the cage door lock, then at the sign over the door. "This is an interesting choice," he says to Luigi, pulling the key from his overalls. He points to the inscription on the key. "'Use once, then discard.' What should we do?"

Mario and Luigi back toward the doorway. Mario holds the key, ready to open the door.

Bowser becomes hysterical. "Don't leave me with that ape," he begs. "He'll turn me into turtle wax." Then the turtle begins to sob. "I'll do anything. I'll tell you where I hid all the coins in the mushroom world. I'll tell you the location of all the warp zones. I'll even be nice to the mushroom people. Honest I will."

Mario turned to Luigi. "Do we free the cowardly turtle or take the door?"

Junior lumbers closer and closer.

Luigi looks at his brother and says, "We both know the answer to that question. Let's move fast."

The Super Mario Bros. get 10 points.

If you think Mario and Luigi should free Bowser, turn to page 34.

If you think Mario and Luigi should unlock the door, turn to page 43.

29

"Too many!" shouts Mario. "Start climbing."

Mario and Luigi climb the vines with renewed vigor. "It's amazing how much energy you have when there's a large angry ape chasing you," pants Luigi.

They manage to put some distance between themselves and Donkey Kong Jr., mainly because he is distracted by a large tasty bunch of bananas.

Soon the vines are replaced by hanging chains. At the bottom of each chain is a large padlock. "This must be the heavy metal part of the jungle," comments Luigi.

Finally, they reach another platform. "This is the final climb," says Mario.

"Good," says Luigi, catching his breath.

"Did I tell you we have to do this part pushing a lock up the chain?" asks Mario.

Luigi looks at his brother in disbelief. "Who makes these things up?" he asks.

"Don't ask me," replies Mario. "I guess old video games never die." He starts pushing a lock up the nearest chain. Luigi follows on another chain.

"Oh, one more thing. Did I tell you about the chain chompers?" asks Mario.

Luigi just stares at his brother.

"Hit them with your lock," says Mario.

The warning comes just in time. Chain chompers start descending the links above them. Luigi takes Mario's advice and bonks them repeatedly with his lock.

"Actually, this is fun," says Luigi as they approach the top platform. "I'm kind of sad to see it end."

"I could press RESET," says Mario. He hits the last chain chomper and climbs onto the final level of Donkey Kong Jr.

Luigi follows. "Maybe next time."

The Super Mario Bros. get 15 points.
Turn to page 32.

30

"**Y**ou always were a fraidy-cat when it came to Phantos," says Mario.

"I just hate floating heads," explains Luigi. "I always think they're looking for a body and they have their eyes on mine."

The two plumbers move quickly to the other side of the jar and hide from the oncoming swarm of Beezos. The swarm zooms past their hiding place and keeps going out of sight over a hill.

Luigi looks up and points to a door in the jar's side. "It's latched with a double-bolt lock," says Luigi, pointing to the device below the door handle. The two bolts face each other with their threads interlocked. "The instructions say to pick a destination and turn the bolts."

"Another door! Just what we need." exclaims Mario, disgusted.

"Let's open the door and see where it goes. Then we can decide what's next. I already have this thing figured out."

The bolts are connected to a pointer. The arrow now points to a sign that says, THIS WAY TO THE BOSS BUFONIDAE. If the two bolts move farther apart when they are turned, the pointer will move right, toward a sign that reads, THIS WAY TO THE SIMIAN MORASS. If they move closer together, the pointer will move toward a third sign. It reads, THIS WAY TO THE GRAND EGRESS.

Above the lock is a set of instructions. The last line says, 'Twist once to open.'

"This looks more complicated than the sprinkler system you designed for the king's hedge maze," complains Mario.

"Actually, it's simple," says Luigi. "We just grab both ends of the bolts and twist once, like the sign says."

"But which way do we twist?" asks Mario.

Solve this puzzle to see what happens next:

• Look at the illustration on the next page and decide which way Mario and Luigi should turn the bolts. The door will open to the appropriate location.

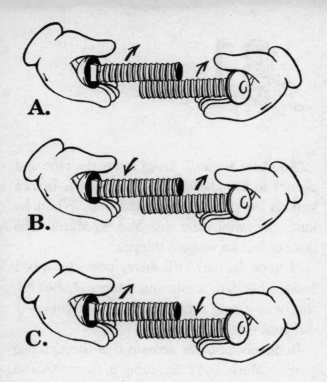

A.

B.

C.

The Super Mario Bros. get 10 points.

If Luigi turns the bolts as shown in illustration A, turn to page 48.

If he turns them as shown in illustration B, turn to page 3.

If he twists them as shown in illustration C, turn to page 111.

31

"*AaaAaaaAaaaa!*" Luigi grabs the vine and swings to the platform. He lets out a Tarzan yell as he sails through the air. When he lands, he swings the vine back to Mario. His brother follows without the yell.

"I hope Jr. isn't still angry over the way I treated his dad," comments Mario. "After all, that was a long time ago and in a completely different video-game system."

Suddenly, another scream rips through the jungle. Mario and Luigi jump to their feet and cover their ears. The sound is a cross between Tarzan's yell and the screech their aunt Maria makes when they walk on her newly waxed floor.

"Heeere's Junior," says Luigi, looking down toward the source of the sound.

"I guess apes never forget," responds Mario.

Below them a very mean-looking ape is making its way up the vines toward them.

"We have two choices," says Mario. "We can try to bonk him with coconuts or try to out-climb him on the vines."

"How many coconuts does it take to bonk Donkey Kong Jr.?" asks Luigi.

"This is no time for riddles," says Mario.

"It's a serious question," protests Luigi.

Use what the Super Mario Bros. know about bonking to decide what to do next:

• It takes more than 100 coconuts to bonk Donkey Kong Jr. into submission.

• The Mario Bros. can each throw 5 coconuts every 10 seconds.

• Donkey Kong Jr. will reach the platform in 100 seconds.

The Super Mario Bros. get 15 points.

If Mario and Luigi bonk Donkey Kong Jr., turn to page 84.

If they can't bonk him, turn to page 61.

32

Luigi takes his finger off the button marked B. The door begins to glow, then opens a crack.

"Come on," says Luigi.

The door swings wide open and both plumbers' eyes grow wide. They are staring into the muzzle of an Autobomb. Sitting atop the mobile canon is a Shyguy wearing sunglasses and a very radical robe.

"Excellent!" exclaims the Shydude.

"Kaboom!" exclaims the Autobomb as it fires from point-blank range.

The circling Beezos swoop down onto two empty plumber's caps.

Game Over!

33

"Therefore, your head is bigger," says Luigi in a dazzling display of logic.

Mario's head is spinning. "Okay, but are you sure?" he says, shaking his head.

"Positive," replies Luigi. "The facts speak for themselves."

"If you say so," grumbles Mario. He removes his hat and hands it over to Wart. "Gnarly," says the toad. "Here's the most electronic opener."

Mario takes the garage door opener and puts it into his overalls pocket. "Thanks, Large Green Dude," he says politely.

"You can exit via my secret passage," says Wart as he hops down from his pedestal and opens a door behind one of his posters.

"Thanks," says Luigi as he ducks into the tunnel.

"Party on," answers Wart in farewell.

The plumbers climb through a secret tunnel

out the back of Wart's cave. The tunnel is very narrow, but they can see a light at the other end.

"I hope that's not an oncoming Fryguy," says Mario as he crawls toward the light. Finally they reach the end of the tunnel. A door blocks their exit. Luckily, it's not locked. They step outside onto a path and the open sky of Subcon. Directly in front of them is a giant garage door.

The Super Mario Bros. get 15 points.
Mario now has the garage door opener.
Turn to page 114.

34

"**D**on't worry, little brother," says Mario from the top rim of the jar. "I won't let the big bad Phanto get you."

"I'll get you for that," shouts Luigi as he follows Mario into the jar.

The two plumbers land on a ledge at the top of the container. It's surprisingly light and roomy inside. The walls are a series of ledges that form a checkerboard.

"I wonder how these jars can have more room inside than outside," marvels Mario.

"It's Subcon logic," explains Luigi. "You see, the nature of the space-time continuum is altered by the presence of dream resonance in Subcon. The resulting warp in the fabric of the universe creates the illusion of mega-space which produces . . ."

Before Mario falls asleep from Luigi's explanation, the lid of the jar opens. They hear the voice of Dr. Von Fungenstein.

"Welcome to Phanto Chess," he intones. "To escape, you must evade the Phanto and reach the door at the base of the jar. Every time you move one square, the Phanto moves one square toward you. You cannot move diagonally and neither can the Phanto, except that the Phanto must move diagonally to get you. If you reach the door safely, you may leave."

Mario and Luigi look at each other. "This is a cinch," says Mario. "He must not know that we're the reigning Sewer Chess Champs of the mushroom worlds."

"Let's make this interesting," says Luigi. "I'll bet you a large peanut butter and sardine pizza that I can get us out of here in seven moves."

"No way," replies Mario. "It will take at least eight moves to do it. You're on!"

"Watch," says Luigi, and starts moving.

Solve the puzzle on the opposite page to see what happens next:

• Study the Phanto Chess puzzle. Follow the rules and get Mario and Luigi to the exit in the least number of moves while avoiding the Phanto.

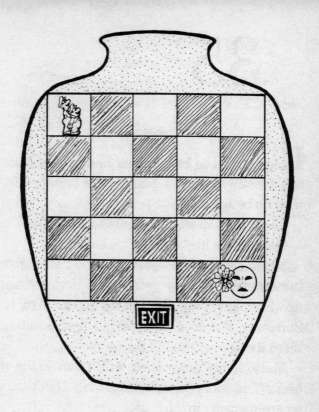

The Super Mario Bros. get 10 points.

If you think Luigi can do it in seven moves, turn to page 101.

If you think it will take more than seven moves, turn to page 3.

35

Luigi grabs the garage door handle and gives it a twist. It doesn't budge. He tries again, with no better luck.

"Give me a hand," he grunts to Mario.

Mario claps his hands. Luigi frowns.

Mario walks to the door. Together they give the handle a mighty twist. The door swings upward, carrying the Mario Bros. with it. Suddenly, it comes to a jarring halt, sending them flying over the hill into a pit.

Mario comes down hard, with Luigi on top of him. The older plumber scowls. "Isn't this where we came in?" he asks.

"Not quite," says Luigi, pointing to a door. They open it and step through.

The Super Mario Bros. get 10 points.
Turn to page 21.

36

"We have a better chance if we split up," thinks Luigi. He races to the end of the platform and takes the next ladder up.

Barrels plummet past both plumbers as they climb. But they get into the rhythm of the oncoming obstacles and move quickly to the third level of the scaffold.

A cascade of barrels thunders toward Mario as he nears a ladder at the end of the scaffold. He clears the missiles in one giant leap—and comes down squarely on Luigi's hat, just as Luigi reaches the top of a ladder. Mario loses his balance.

Grabbing for his aching noggin, Luigi clutches Mario's foot just as his brother begins to fall. Mario's weight pulls Luigi over. He dangles precariously from the ladder, held by only one foot.

Oof! Mario slams against the scaffold. As the two brothers dangle in space, a door appears in midair above them. Dr. Von Fungenstein pops his head through the doorway.

"This is no fun," he snarls. "You can't die on the first challenge. I'll tell you what. If you can solve this puzzle, I'll save your grimy necks. If you can't, then you deserve what you get. All you have to do is tell me the last word in this puzzle."

A ladder with words above the rungs appears in front of the hanging plumbers. The last rung is missing. Below them a door opens into space.

Luigi strains his neck to look at the puzzle. Mario can't see it, because he can't bend his neck back that far.

"I think I know the answer," says Luigi.

His foot begins to slip. "Well, what are you waiting for?" shouts Mario.

As the Mario Bros. begin to fall, Luigi shouts out his solution.

Solve the puzzle below to decide what word Luigi shouts as he and Mario fall through the door.

- Read the hints next to each rung of the ladder.
- Change one letter at a time from the previous word until you reach the bottom. The last word is the one Luigi shouts.

DROP

CROP

Something farmers grow: COOP

A place where chickens live: CORP

Short for corporation: CORE

The center of an apple: CARE

I don't ____!: CAVE

An underground chamber: SAVE

What you're supposed to do with money:

The Super Mario Bros. get 10 points.

✶ If Luigi shouts "SAVE", turn to page 106.

If he hollers "SAFE", turn to page 118.

77

37

"We can't desert the princess," Luigi finishes his brother's thought.

"Of course not," says his older brother. "What do you take us for? Koopas? Besides, I have something that Mr. Kong can't resist. When I distract him, run for it."

Mario pulls a brown banana left over from Tuesday's lunch from his overalls. He waves the smelly mess in Donkey Kong's face.

The ape roars again and prepares to smash the two plumbers to smithereens. But as the barrel starts to descend onto their collective heads, the ape's expression changes from anger to surprise. He totters and begins to fall forward. Mario and Luigi leap straight up as the massive gorilla plunges headfirst over the edge and falls into the mist below.

Mario and Luigi land on the girder and tumble forward. "That was some powerful banana," says Luigi in amazement.

"Banana, schmanana," pronounces a confident female voice. "I gave him the royal crown treatment right in the backside." The surprised plumbers see a triumphant Princess Toadstool holding her golden crown in one of her fists.

"Now, will someone tell me what's going on here?" she says indignantly, glaring at both plumbers.

Turn to page 96.

79

38

Wart opens his mouth with a loud croak.

Luigi quickly pulls a turnip from his overalls and heaves it into Wart's jaws.

The toad swallows, turns pink, then spits the turnip back at Luigi.

"I guess he's learned something since last time," says Luigi anxiously.

"Run!" shouts Mario. The plumbers rush out the door and scamper down the hall. Behind them, Wart's foot slaps against the floor as his skateboard gathers speed.

The tunnel deadends at a locked door. Mario and Luigi struggle to open the latch.

The sound of racing wheels becomes a roar behind them. In a green flash, Wart takes the skateboard aloft and does a beautiful windmill turn on top of them.

Game Over!

39

Mario reaches for the door handle and opens the first door. He and Luigi step through.

"Oh, no!" groans Luigi.

The two plumbers are in a large classroom. At the head of the class stands Dr. Von Fungenstein.

"I'm Professor Von Fungenstein," he introduces himself. "Take your seats. You have a lot to learn before you take the makeup exam."

Game Over!

40

As the elevator moves relentlessly to the top, the two plumbers look around for some means of escape. "This looks like a sure Game Over," says Mario.

"What a bummer!" says Luigi glumly.

Suddenly, a door appears in midair. The brothers look hopefully at each other.

The floating door bursts open and Dr. Von Fungenstein pokes his evil face through the doorway. Thick fog seeps out around him, quickly engulfing the Mario Bros. and the elevator.

"Going up?" asks the doctor, then laughs loudly at his own joke. "I think I can help. All you have to do is solve this puzzle and I'll let you escape through the door." The doctor holds up a sheet of paper with a puzzle on it.

Mario and Luigi stare at the puzzle, as the shadow of the scaffold falls over them.

Solve this puzzle to see what happens next:

• Help the Mario Bros. figure out how many rectangles are contained in the scaffolding in the picture.

✳ **If you think there are 20 or more, turn to page 44.**

✕ **If you think there are fewer than 20, turn to page 100.**

41

"We have enough," says Mario. "Just start throwing before he gets any closer."

"Coconuts away!" yells Luigi, letting fly with the first barrage. The two brothers grab coconuts from the trees and throw them down at the rapidly climbing ape.

Coconuts bounce off Donkey Kong Jr.'s head. The more they throw, the angrier the ape gets—and the faster he climbs.

"This is going nowhere fast," says Mario. "We'd better make a break for it."

As the plumbers jump for the vines, Junior reaches the platform. The ape grabs the plumbers and holds them out over the edge.

He smiles a goofy monkey smile as he lets go and gives the plumbers a ride to the bottom of the jungle—without a vine!

Game Over!

42

"Subcon," Mario says hollowly.

Luigi looks around at the open airy landscape. "I always liked Subcon," he says, admiring the blue sky, white clouds, green hills, and palm trees.

"The perfect place for a vacation," adds Mario. "I don't even mind the constant attacks from Shyguys, Tweeters, Snifits, and Ninjis. But that never-ending organ music drives me batty."

As if on cue, the music changes pitch. Two red-clad Shyguys approach the plumbers. Immediately, Mario bends down and plucks a clump of grass growing nearby. When he pulls up the grass, a smiling turnip emerges from the ground. Mario hurls the vegetable at the leading Shyguy. "Remember to eat your vegetables," he says coyly.

The Shyguy recoils from the impact of the turnip and collides with its companion. Both monsters bounce once, turn upside down and disappear into the ground.

"Shyguys sure hate veggies," says Luigi, pulling another turnip from the ground.

"Did you notice anything different about them?" asks Mario.

"Well, they were wearing sunglasses over their masks and they had on Hawaiian robes," says Luigi. "Nothing unusual," he adds.

"I know Subcon is strange, but surfer Shyguys are ridiculous," mutters Mario.

"It's more like Surfcon than Subcon," comments Luigi, smiling at his own joke.

The two plumbers trot along a grassy path. They encounter more beach-bum Shyguys and several Tweeters dressed in surfer shorts. As they get deeper into Subcon the dream demons become more plentiful, but with the help of the local vegetable crop, the Mario Bros. handle them easily.

Luigi takes the lead while Mario trails behind, lost in thought. Finally, the red-clad plumber calls out to his younger brother. "I remember a warp zone up ahead. If we can find a magic potion, we can take a shortcut to the end of Subcon."

They approach a cliff and look over the edge. "The warp zone is down there," says Mario.

"How do we get down?" asks Luigi. "We don't learn to fly until the next adventure."

Without warning, a large group of black figures approaches. They look like little devils with big eyes. They are moving very fast, directly toward the Mario Bros.

"A swarm of Ninjis!" exclaims Luigi. The Ninjis are dressed completely in black, as usual, except that now they are wearing black bicycle pants emblazoned with yellow palm trees and red Ree-Bob-Omb sneakers.

"There are too many of them," says Luigi. "Our only hope is to jump."

The Super Mario Bros. get 20 points.
If Luigi has the parasol, turn to page 89.
If Luigi has no parasol, turn to page 118.

43

"I don't think we can make it," shouts Mario over the hum of the Beezo bombers.

"So duck already," screams Luigi.

They duck as the Beezos swoop past.

As they stand up again, a red streak zooms over their barrel and into the water.

"Trouter!" Mario jumps to avoid the deadly fish from Subcon's waterfalls. When he comes down, he lands hard on his end of the barrel and sends Luigi flying into the water. His brother disappears with a splash.

But Mario has little time to regret his actions. Another Trouter flashes out of the waterfall, hitting him between the eyes.

"What a way to go," he gasps. "Felled by a fish!"

Game Over!

44

As they plunge through the air, Luigi pulls the parasol from his pocket. He presses the button and the umbrella unfolds with a snap. The two plumbers float softly to the ground.

They are standing in a deep valley. The hills are too steep to climb.

"We're trapped!" groans Luigi.

"Not so," responds Mario cheerfully. He pulls up a tuft of grass. Out of the ground pops a bottle filled with red liquid.

He holds the bottle over his head triumphantly. "Magic potion!"

"Let's get moving," says Luigi. "The Beezos might return at any moment."

Mario throws the bottle against the side of the hill. It disappears in a twinkle and is replaced by a shiny red door. He turns the handle, giving the door a hard shove. It doesn't budge. "Give me a hand, Luigi," he says.

Luigi applauds.

Mario gives his brother a glare that could stop a Triclyde dead in its tracks.

"It's locked," says Luigi. "With a lace lock. It looks like shoelaces on the outside, but you can't untie it. To unlock the door you have to figure out what the other side looks like."

"I'm great at these puzzles," says Mario enthusiastically.

"Excuse me, but you can't even tie your shoes," replies Luigi. "Let me handle this."

Below the lock are two large buttons. Each has a shoelace pattern drawn on it.

Luigi inspects the door. "Which button matches the other side of the laces?"

He bites his lip, then quickly presses a button.

Solve the puzzle on the opposite page to find out which button Luigi chose:

• Study the pictures below. The top drawing shows the lace lock from the front. The buttons below it show what the laces might look like from the back. Choose the one you think is correct.

The Super Mario Bros. get 15 points.

If you think Luigi pressed button A,
turn to page 21.

If you think he pressed button B,
turn to page 68.

45

Mario swings the white door open and stops dead in his tracks. Luigi walks up beside him. The two plumbers stare at a huge metal scaffold on the other side of the door. "Is that what I think it is?" asks Luigi.

Mario just gulps. He's been here before.

"It's just as you described it," says Luigi excitedly. "Angled metal girders, ladders between levels, elevators moving up and down, vats of flaming oil, and empty barrels falling from above. This is great!"

"No," says Mario, "this is Donkey Kong."

Luigi leaps through the door. Mario follows, dodging a barrel as it whizzes past his head. The top of the metal scaffold is out of sight, but there is no doubt who is raining destruction down on them.

"Is there really a giant ape up there throwing barrels on us?" asks Luigi as he dodges yet another falling barrel.

"Would I lie to you about a thing like that?" replies Mario. Immediately, they are assaulted by more barrels rolling down the tilted beams of the metal structure. They jump in unison to avoid the assault.

"I thought I was done with that big ape forever," says Mario. "I guess I must have quit before reaching the last level. But this time I'll fix him for good." He runs along the girder toward the first ladder.

Luigi runs to catch up, shouting, "Do we stick together or do we split up?"

The Super Mario Bros. get 20 points.

If you think the Mario Bros. should split up, turn to page 75.

If you think Luigi should stay with his brother, turn to page 13.

46

"There is no doubt that you have the biggest head," says Luigi, concluding his logical analysis.

"There's no way I'm falling for that," says Mario emphatically.

Instead, Mario applies his own logic. He insists that Luigi is smarter than him, therefore his head must be larger. Luigi reminds Mario of his status as Hero Extraordinaire. "We are the Mario Bros. after all," he argues.

Finally, Mario says, "There's only one way to solve this. We have to do Rag, Tin Snips, Wrench."

Luigi nods. The two brothers clench their fists and shake their hands three times. On the third shake, Luigi holds out a single finger, Wrench. Mario opens his hand and extends all five fingers, Rag.

"Rag beats Wrench, I win," exults Mario. "Give him your hat."

Luigi reluctantly hands his hat to Wart. The giant toad takes it and tries to put the chapeau on his oversized head. But because his head is so large, the hat begins to rip.

Luigi watches his favorite hat disintegrate before his eyes. Finally, he can't contain himself any longer. He grabs the hat from the fatheaded reptile.

"I changed my mind," he shouts as he tries to repair the damage. "Why don't we just give him the vegetable treatment? Feed him a few turnips and he'll explode."

Mario frowns at his brother. "I don't think we should do him in when all we have to do is give him a hat. Let's try reason."

The Super Mario Bros. get 10 points.

If you think Mario and Luigi should feed the toad, turn to page 80.

If you think they should try to reason with him, turn to page 26.

47

"**I** was just about to ask that question," replies Mario, regaining his composure.

"One minute I'm in my room in the palace, and the next thing I know, I'm on top of this tower being chased by a gorilla," Princess Toadstool explains. "I had no choice but to take refuge in that cage. The key was in the lock, so I took it into the cage with me and locked the door behind me.

"Lucky for me you two showed up to 'rescue' me," she adds sarcastically.

"That gorilla is Mario's old friend Donkey Kong," Luigi explains. He goes on to tell the princess how Dr. Von Fungenstein transported them here with the Doors to Doom machine and how Mario and Luigi are trying to stop him. Luigi finishes on a dismal note. "Now we're stuck here with no way down."

"Except the door that Donkey Kong came through," adds Mario. "Let's check it out."

The three adventurers walk toward the other end of the steel platform. Mario and Luigi leap over an odd-looking section of the girder almost without thinking. Luigi turns to tell Princess Toadstool to watch her step.

"Watch out, your Highness. That could be a trap," Luigi says, just as the princess's royal foot touches the unusual girder. Suddenly a trap door flies open. The mushroom monarchess falls through in a pink blur.

"Yeow!" screams the princess as she drops beneath the platform.

"Princess!" cries Luigi. He grabs for her, but it's too late. The trap door slams shut with a solid clunk.

Luigi jumps onto the girder in a desperate attempt to follow the princess. But this time the door doesn't open. Mario rushes to his brother's side and leaps onto the door with him. Still nothing happens.

The two desperate plumbers bounce up and down on the girder until both are out of breath. Finally, they stop to rest. As they stand looking at the trapdoor, the expression on Mario's face changes from exhaustion to anger. "Listen," he says to Luigi. The sickening laughter of Dr. Von Fungenstein echoes up through the trap door.

"I'll get that Dr. Von Fungicide if it's the last thing I do," says Luigi through clenched teeth.

"That's *Fungenstein,* and there's no point beating our boots against this door," says Mario. "Let's try to find a way off this over-sized Erector Set."

They turn to the door at the end of the platform. It's locked with a set of five cogs. Each has eight letters around its edges.

Mario looks at the sign above the lock. "The instructions say, 'What you spell is where you go. Turn the first wheel and you'll know.'"

"Spelling was never my strong point," says Mario, reaching for the cog on the far left. "But here goes." He twists the cog.

Solve the puzzle below to see what happens next:

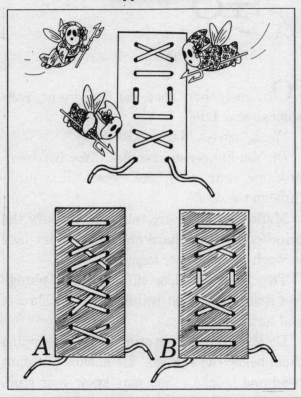

If you think Luigi twists the cog to the right, turn to page 3.

If you think Luigi twists the cog to the right, turn to page 3.

If you think he twists it to the left, turn to page 85.

48

"**O**bviously there are fewer than twenty rectangles," says Luigi.

"Yeah," agrees Mario. "Obviously."

Dr. Von Fungenstein smiles. "You boys really know your stuff," he says. "Just jump through the door."

Mario and Luigi are reluctant to leave the princess, but they have no choice. They leap through the open door together.

They clear the door sill easily and plunge feet first into a giant boiling pot of mushroom and turtle soup.

Dr. Von Fungenstein stirs the broth, sending them below the surface. He shakes his giant head and laughs. "You may know your stuff, but you sure don't know your math!"

Game Over!

49

Luigi turns the knob and opens the black door. He stares into utter darkness. Mario joins him at the entrance. "What do you think is out there?" asks the younger brother.

Before Mario can answer, the door slams shut behind them, shoving both plumbers into the dark chamber.

The floor abruptly disappears beneath them, and they fall for several seconds. When they land they are on the top level of a green, wedding-cake shaped hill. The grass on the hillside forms a wavy pattern. Luigi looks down at the ledges that form the layers below them. A hooded pink figure patrols the next ledge down. The figure is wearing a white mask and moving back and forth along the ledge in an unending cycle.

Luigi points down at the pink sentry. "A Shyguy," he says to Mario. "Let's jump over it. Geronimo!"

Mario and Luigi leap over the Shyguy, landing on a lower level of the terraced hill. As Mario looks around, his expression grows gloomier by the minute. "I think we've been here before," he says.

"I hope you're still dreaming," responds Luigi. "Because this sure looks like the entrance to Subcon, the Land of Dreams."

The Super Mario Bros. get 15 points.
Turn to page 85.

50

Luigi moves ahead of his older brother and steps through the door without looking back. The door slams behind him.

He looks over his shoulder at the sound. He's standing in the hall of the Mario Bros.' Brooklyn plumbing shop, at the entrance to his room. The door behind him is closed.

When he turns around, Mario is walking down the hallway toward a blank wall. He is obviously sleepwalking.

Luigi grabs his sleepwalking brother just as he is about to crash into the wall. Mario awakens with a start.

"I just had the strangest dream," he says sleepily.

"Me too," says Luigi. "But now I can't remember what it was."

Game Over!

51

"Hold on a minute," says Mario as he pulls the garage door opener from his overalls. "I knew this would be worth it." He holds the garage door opener in his outstretched hand and presses the button. Nothing happens. He presses again with the same result.

Mario is about to throw the opener at the door when Luigi reaches out and takes it from him. He looks at it, then smiles.

"You were holding it backwards," he says. Turning the opener around, he presses the button again. The enormous door swings open. Mario and Luigi jump backward to avoid being hit.

"Holy pipe wrenches!" exclaims Mario as he sees what's inside.

They stare into a large garage laboratory, complete with beakers of boiling liquid connected by tubes, rows of shelves lined with bottles containing animal, mineral and vegetable powders, the largest assortment of electronic paraphernalia that they have ever seen, and a stale baloney sandwich on one counter top.

Standing in the middle of the lab is Dr. Von Fungenstein. He turns and smiles at Mario and Luigi. "Glad you could make it," he says. "Step right in. What took you so long?"

The Super Mario Bros. get 15 points.
Turn to page 115.

The plumber brothers nosedive through the air.

"Save . . . mmgphmm!" Luigi is trying to say something, but a large bug has flown into his mouth. He spits it out, disgusted.

"Save yourself!" yells Mario.

Splat! They finally land in a pile of grass and old banana peels. Vines hang all around them. The vegetation is so thick that they can see only a few feet in any direction. Lying on their backs, recovering from the fall, they see dozens of Snapjaws descending from the vines toward them.

The creatures are all mouth. When they reach the bottom of their vine, they turn around and climb up again. "Those snappers are easy to avoid," instructs Mario. "Just keep your eyes open.

"It's been a while since I was here," he continues, "but this is definitely Donkey Kong Jr.'s jungle."

"Isn't this where you captured that giant ape, Donkey Kong, and his son came after you?" asks Luigi.

"Yeah, and he wasn't too happy with the outcome of that game," replies Mario.

"How do we get out of here before Junior shows up?" asks Luigi.

Mario looks around. "The only way out of here is up. On the top level of this world there's a door back to Brooklyn. It opens onto the Botanic Gardens."

The Mario Bros. start climbing the nearest Snapjawless vine. It's hard work in the jungle heat, wearing denim overalls.

"That platform looks like a good place to take a break," Mario says after a while, pointing to a floating stage not far away from the vine they are climbing. "We'll have to swing over to it, though. I hope you're not afraid to play Tarzan."

"I'll just grab this other vine and show you who's afraid," boasts Luigi.

"Wait!" says Mario. "We'd better use another vine. That one isn't long enough."

Solve this puzzle and help Mario and Luigi decide which vine is longer:

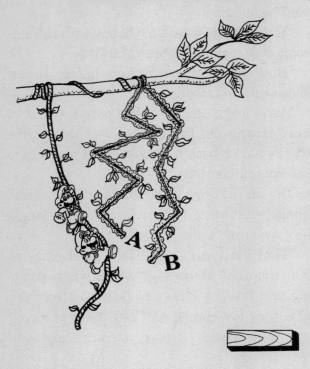

The Super Mario Bros. get 20 points.

If you think Mario and Luigi should choose vine A, turn to page 66.

If you think they should choose vine B, turn to page 7.

53

"We can't give him the correct answer and harm the princess," says Mario.

"I think there's another way out," replies Luigi, lowering his voice. The brothers whisper to each other for a moment, then turn to the smiling scientist.

"We've thought it over, and the answer we're going to give you is, 'fewer than twenty rectangles,'" says Luigi. Both plumbers smile knowingly at the evil lab fungus.

The doctor turns red in the face. "You know the answer! You're just protecting that wretched girl!" he shouts wildly.

As he raves on, the two brothers initiate part B of their plan.

Mario quickly jumps onto his brother's shoulders. This gives him the height he needs. Without hesitating, he bends his knees and leaps through the air, just as the mad doctor slams the door.

Mario's head and the door arrive at the door frame at the same instant. *Crack!* The door bounces open and Mario falls. Instinctively, the dazed plumber grabs the threshold. He hangs from the door with his feet dangling in midair.

"Good timing," shouts Luigi. He leaps off the lift and grabs Mario's legs. They swing like trapeze artists from the door.

"I think we can swing to the scaffolding from here," says Luigi, pumping his legs to increase their motion.

"Give me a break," groans Mario. "I'm not made of rubber." Then he says, "Maybe we should climb up through the door and try to catch Dr. F. But we'd better move fast. I'm losing my grip."

The Super Mario Bros. get 15 points.

If you think Mario and Luigi should swing to the scaffold, turn to page 5.

If you think they should climb through the doorway, turn to page 18.

54

"'GRAND EGRESS.' I like that. I'll just give the bolts a little twist, like so," declares Luigi.

As he turns the bolts, the jar vibrates. In a blinding flash the door swings open, revealing a tranquil landscape. A warm, gentle breeze blows through the doorway.

"What did I tell you?" says Luigi as he leans forward to take a peek. Mario steps up behind him.

Suddenly the balmy breeze turns to a harsh, hot wind. The heat intensifies and becomes unbearable. *Whoosh,* a collossal Fryguy engulfs Mario and Luigi. The living fireball explodes into a million sparks, leaving two piles of charred ashes, one green and the other red.

Game Over!

55

Mario and Luigi talk it over. "I think we should ask them what they would do if it were up to them," says Mario.

Luigi shrugs. "Sounds good to me," he replies.

Mario turns to the guard on the left and asks the question. The Ninji replies in a squeaky voice as it bounces up and down, "My door is the one I'd choose. Much better than the other door, much better."

Luigi asks the other Ninji the same question. Its response is identical to its brother's.

Mario and Luigi look at each other. "I guess it was the other question," says Mario. He turns to ask the first Ninji the other question. But the Ninjis are already opening the doors.

A dull roar resounds from the passage behind one of the doors. Mario and Luigi step up to see what is making the sound.

Their eyes grow wide as a giant toad riding

a skateboard bears down on them at breakneck speed. The two brothers jump together to avoid the oncoming skatetoad.

But this toad knows his stuff. He reaches down, grabs the nose of his board, and lifts off. The airborne toad collides with the Mario Bros., sending them flying against the walls of the tunnel.

"Radical!" shouts the toad as it zooms down the ramp. The sound of racing wheels is all Mario and Luigi hear before everything goes black.

Game Over!

113

56

The garage door is imbedded in the hillside. Strange sounds come from the other side.

"Too bad we didn't drive," says Mario.

"I'd hate to see the car that fits in that garage," says Luigi. "But let's go in anyway." He reaches for the handle.

The Super Mario Bros. get 25 points.

If Mario has the garage door opener, turn to page 104.

If he doesn't have the garage door opener, turn to page 74.

57

Mario and Luigi look at each other, then warily enter the lab.

"I've been expecting you," Dr. Von Fungenstein says cheerfully.

"What's next, Dr. Von Fungenstein?" asks Luigi. "Is this your little soup kitchen?"

"That's Fungen—" Mario starts to say. Then he realizes his brother got it right.

"You can relax," says the doctor. "You see, I told you boys a little fib. I'm not trying to take over the mushroom world, or any other world. Actually, I work for the Mushroom King and Princess Toadstool."

Luigi looks at Mario. "Let's jump him. This guy is as looney as a wild mushroom."

"Let me explain," begs Von Fungenstein.

Mario looks at the doctor. "Let's hear what he has to say. I have a funny feeling he may be telling the truth."

Luigi shakes his head. "You're so trusting."

Then he looks back at the doctor. "This better be good," he says firmly. "One false move and you're mushroom mush."

The bespectacled mushroom goes on. "My name is *Professor* Von Fungenstein. I'm the Mushroom Kingdom's chief scientist. I was commissioned by the Royal Academy of Mushroom Science to administer a test to the famous Mario Bros. Every decade, or so, the R.A.M.S. presents an award for outstanding heroism, bravery, ingenuity, moral character, and overall good looks. This year you two are the nominees."

Luigi is very skeptical. "So you try to do us in as a reward," he says. "That makes sense." Then he yells, "If you're a whacked-out mushroom!"

The professor chuckles. "The whole adventure was a test to see if you were worthy of the award.

"Don't take my word for it," Dr. Von Fungenstein goes on. "Here's my official royal commission." He hands Mario a large proclamation with the royal seal at the base. Mario looks it over, then hands it to Luigi.

"I think he's serious," says Mario.

After examining the document, Luigi is forced to agree.

"How did we do?" asks Mario.

"I just tallied your score," replies the professor. He gives Mario a score sheet.

Dr. Von Fungenstein steps to the wall and pulls back a curtain. Behind it are three doors. "Check your score, then step through the appropriate door," he says.

Luigi looks at Mario skeptically.

Mario shrugs and heads for one of the doors. Luigi follows closely behind.

Help the Mario Bros. choose which door to go through. Tally your score on page 121, then select the correct door.

The Super Mario Bros. get 50 points.

If Mario and Luigi scored less than 200, turn to page 81.

If they scored between 210 and 400, turn to page 103.

If they scored more than 400, turn to page 19.

58

"Yeow!" shouts Mario.

"I knew it wasn't safe," sighs Luigi.

The two plumbers plunge through space. They land on the floor back in Dr. Von Fungenstein's small room.

The doctor reappears in the door above them. "I expected more from both of you," he says, shaking his head disappointedly.

He pulls a large lever just inside the door. Mario and Luigi hear a grinding sound as the walls begin to close in on them.

"You guessed right about the plumber sauce," laughs the doctor, slamming the door shut.

Game Over!

59

Once again, the faint voice cries, "Help!"

"That sounds like Princess Toadstool! The Donkster will just have to wait," Mario says as he leaps through the trapdoor. Luigi follows immediately. They drop quickly and land on another girder. Mario recognizes it immediately. "We're near the top of the scaffold," he says.

"Only in the mushroom worlds can you go down to get to the top," comments Luigi.

The cries for help are much louder now, and they're clearly coming from the next level of the scaffolding.

"I don't see Donkey Kong up there," says Luigi, looking up.

"I always say, 'Never look a gift ape in the mouth,'" quips Mario. "Let's get to the top, save the princess—or whoever is there— and blow this pile of tin." He starts to leap for the elevator that goes to the top of the scaffold.

Luigi grabs Mario's overalls from behind and

pulls his anxious brother to a halt. "Take a look over there," he says, pointing to a nearby platform. A blue parasol hangs above the scaffolding.

"Isn't that the magic umbrella you told me about?" asks Luigi. "It could be useful. I say we get it, then rush to the rescue."

"Don't be ridiculous!" cries Mario. "We're too close to the top to stop for a bumbershoot. Besides, we don't know when Donkey Kong might show up."

The Super Mario Bros. get 10 points.

If you think Mario and Luigi should take the elevator, turn to page 36.

If you think Mario and Luigi should try to retrieve the parasol, turn to page 16.

Drip by Drip Scorecard

Circle each object as you collect it.

Keep track of your score here:

Now, use this chart to find out how you did on Dr. Von Fungenstein's test of heroism, bravery, ingenuity, moral character, and overall good looks. Tally your points, then check your rating on the chart.

Did you visit the visit Donkey Kong, Donkey Kong Jr., and Subcon? Did you rescue the princess and save Bowser? Did you find the key and the parasol?

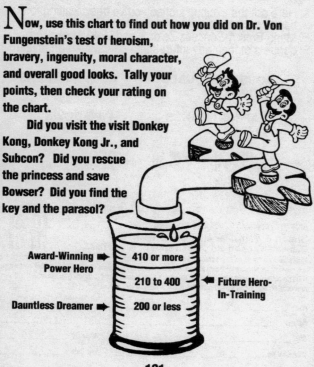

Award-Winning Power Hero ➡ 410 or more

210 to 400 ⬅ Future Hero-In-Training

Dauntless Dreamer ➡ 200 or less